Fair Cow

Written and illustrated by
Leslie Helakoski

Marshall Cavendish Children

Library of Congress Cataloging-in-Publication Data
Helakoski, Leslie.
Fair cow / by Leslie Helakoski. — 1st ed.
p. cm.
Summary: Effie the cow dreams of winning a blue ribbon at
the state fair, while her best friend Petunia advises her to give up
all that she truly enjoys in order to prepare for the big day.
ISBN 978-0-7614-5684-1
[1. Cows—Fiction. 2. Agricultural exhibitions—Fiction.
3. Individuality—Fiction.] I. Title.
PZ7.H37275Fai 2010
[E]—dc22
2009004789

The illustrations are rendered in
acrylic on paper.

Book design by Virginia Pope
Editor: Robin Benjamin

Printed in Malaysia (T)
First edition

10 9 8 7 6 5 4 3 2 1

mc Marshall Cavendish
Children
www.marshallcavendish.us/kids

To my beautiful, bodacious sisters,
Paula, Lea, and Susan

Effie dreamed of being a state-fair cow. She loved living on the farm, grazing in the fields, and giving milk every day. But still . . .

she dreamed of being beautiful, of billowing blue ribbons and big, bodacious barns.

The fair was coming up soon and, luckily,
her friend knew just what to do.

"You're already pretty as a pie," said Petunia. "But if
you want to go to the fair, you need to get gussied up a
bit."

"What do we do first?" asked Effie.

"First, we have to get you in shape," said Petunia.

"What's wrong with my shape?" asked Effie.

"Nothing a little exercise won't fix,"

said Petunia.

Effie did her best. "Can I exercise in the pasture?"

Petunia shook her head. "Too windy," she said. "Just look at your hair."

"What's wrong with my hair?" asked Effie.

"Nothing a few curlers won't fix," said Petunia.

"Ouch," Effie said and headed for the door. "It's so nice outside. Can I sit in the sun?"

Petunia pulled her inside. "Nope. The sun isn't good for your spots."

"What's wrong with my spots?" asked Effie.

"Nothing a little hair dye won't fix,"

said Petunia.

"Can I go to the pond for a drink?" asked Effie.
Petunia gave her a water bottle. "Too messy," she
said. "We have to take care of your hooves."
"What's wrong with my hooves?" asked Effie.

"Nothing a little paint won't fix,"
said Petunia.

Effie swished flies away from the wet paint.

"I've been meaning to talk to you about that tail," said Petunia.

"What's wrong with my tail?" asked Effie.

"Nothing a little glue won't fix," said Petunia.

"Can I still use my tail to shoo flies?" asked Effie.

Petunia shook her head. "Too old-fashioned," she said. "We'll use fly spray."

"Are we done yet?" Effie asked.

"Almost," said Petunia. "You'll have to correct your walk on the way."

"What's wrong with my walk?" asked Effie.

"Nothing a little practice won't fix,"

said Petunia, walking Effie down the road. "Step like this. And don't forget to smile!" she called.

Effie took a deep breath and set off toward the fair.

When Effie arrived, she was escorted to the biggest barn she'd ever laid eyes on.

"Howdy-do," said Effie to the other cows. She stared. "You're all so beautiful."

She looked up. "Your hair is so high."

She looked down. "Your hooves are so shiny."

She looked around. "And your tails are so . . . perfect."

Effie sighed. She felt sick to all four parts of her stomach.

Effie walked with the other cows to the show arena.
"Doesn't that breeze feel good?" Effie asked. She stepped off the path.
The cows gasped. "It'll mess up your hair!"

Effie took a step into the field.
"The grass smells delicious."

The cows shuddered.
"It'll make your teeth green!"
Effie took another step.
"There's fresh water in the pond."
The cows cringed. "It'll make
your belly bloat!"

The cows shook their heads, hurried along the path, and asked each other, "What is wrong with that cow?"

Effie grazed in the sunshine,

cooled off in a mud hole, and

drank from the pond.

And then, with no one else around, she looked at herself . . . and smiled.

Effie clomped into the arena, just in time for the judging. She picked the clover from her teeth, smiled at the judges, and said, "Anybody want some fresh milk?"

The next day, Effie arrived back at the farm. She had dirt on her hooves, tangles in her hair, and . . . a great big blue ribbon around her neck.

Petunia cheered. "Effie, you're a state-fair cow! But how on earth did you do it? You're a mess!"

Effie grinned.

"Nothing a little Effie couldn't fix."